This 2004 edition is published by Gramercy Books, an imprint of Random House Value Publishing,
a division of Random House, Inc., New York, by arrangement with Award Publications Limited.

Gramercy is a registered trademark and the
colophon is a trademark of Random House, Inc.

Random House
New York • Toronto • London • Sydney • Auckland
www.randomhouse.com

Printed and bound in Malaysia

A catalog record for this title is available from the Library of Congress.

ISBN 0-517-22361-9

10 9 8 7 6 5 4 3 2 1

KENNETH GRAHAME'S

The WIND
in the WILLOWS

Adapted by Michael Bishop

Illustrated by
RENE CLOKE

Gramercy Books
New York

CONTENTS

Chapter 1

THE RIVER BANK

ole had been working very hard all morning, spring-cleaning.

First with brooms and dusters, then standing on a little table with a brush and a pot of paint, slap-slap, up-and-down, till he was aching all over.

Suddenly he flung down his brush, said "Bother!" and "Hang spring-cleaning!", and bolted out of the house into the fields outside.

"This is fine," he said to himself. "This is better than painting the house!"

First he met some rabbits as he rambled along the hedgerows.

Soon he found himself by a river. Mole sat down on the grassy bank and then he saw – coming out of a dark hole on the other side – a brown little face with whiskers.

It was the Water Rat.

"Hullo, Mole," said Rat, "I'll come over in my boat to fetch you."

"Do you know, I've never been in a boat before in all my life," said Mole.

"What!" cried Rat. "In that case, let's go down the river together and make a day of it!"

He rowed quickly back across the water with Mole. Rat popped into his hole in the bank and came staggering out a few moments later with a heavy picnic basket.

They rowed down the
river, past the Wild Wood,
as far as an old water mill.
There, Rat brought his boat
alongside the river bank, so that they
could set out the picnic.
"What have we got?" asked
Mole, who was hungry.
"There's chicken and ham
and salad and lemonade and
cake and chocolate
biscuits…"
"Oh, my!" said Mole.

A few minutes later, when they were feeling *much* better and not so hungry, a very wet and furry head suddenly appeared out of the water above the edge of the river bank.

It was Otter.

"You greedy beggars!" he said. "Why didn't you invite me?"

And he set about helping them finish up the picnic.

"All the world seems to be out on the river today," said Otter, wiping his paws on his whiskers.

"Toad's out for one, in his brand new boat, and wearing his new boating clothes."

Just then, Toad flashed into view, rowing rapidly past the water mill. Rat stood up excitedly and waved to him, but Toad just shook his head and rowed on.

By now they had eaten all the food.

Otter was in the middle of telling them a story about Toad – and beginning to feel a bit peckish again – when suddenly he saw a juicy mayfly.

With hardly a splash, he was gone.

So Mole and Rat packed up the picnic things and got back into the boat to go home.

Rat was rowing gently along when Mole said, "Ratty, please, *I* want to row now."

"Not yet, Mole," replied Rat. "It's not as easy as it looks."

But Mole jumped up and grabbed the oars, knocking Rat backwards.

"Stop it!" cried Rat. "You'll have us both over!"

And over they went – SPLOOSH – and they were both struggling in the water.

Rat, of course, was a good swimmer and thought it was very funny.

Having rescued Mole and got him to the river bank to dry off, he plunged back into the water to recover his boat.

Finally, he dived down to the bottom of the river to rescue the picnic basket.

"I *am* sorry, Ratty," said Mole dejectedly.

When they eventually got back home, Rat sat Mole in front of a bright fire to warm him up.

And to cheer him up, he told him river stories until supper-time.

So supper was a very happy meal. And soon afterwards Rat showed a very sleepy Mole upstairs to the best bedroom for the night.

Chapter 2

THE OPEN ROAD

Rat was sitting on the river bank one bright summer morning, singing a song, when Mole said, "Please, Ratty, would you take me to call on Mr. Toad?"

"Why, certainly," said the good-natured Rat. "We'll go in the boat."

"There's Toad Hall," said Rat as they rounded a bend in the river. "Toad is rather rich, you know. Come along and let's find him."

Toad saw them coming across the lawn.

"Hooray!" he cried. "This is splendid. You are the very animals I wanted to see! You've got to help me."

"Is it about rowing?" asked Rat.

"Oh – I've given that up long ago," said Toad airily. "No – I've discovered the real thing. Come with me just as far as the stable yard and you shall see!"

And there it was – a gipsy caravan, shining and new, painted yellow and green with red wheels.

"Who's for a life on the open road – here today, up and off somewhere else tomorrow," said Toad gaily.

"This is the finest cart of its sort that was ever built. Come inside and have a look – planned it all myself!"

Mole was tremendously interested inside, but Rat just sat on the doorstep.

"All complete," said Toad. "Chocolate biscuits, tinned fruit, lemonade – even games to play! You'll find that nothing has been forgotten when we make our start this afternoon."

"Did I hear," said Rat slowly, "something about 'we' and 'start this afternoon'?"

"Oh, come on, Ratty, I want to show you the world!" said Toad.

There was quite an argument, but in the end Toad
was able to persuade Mole and Rat to go with him.

And so, they harnessed Toad's horse and set off
through the lovely countryside.

Friendly passers-by called out "Good day!" to
them, or stopped to say nice things about their
beautiful caravan.

And lots of rabbits sat up on their hind legs and said
"Oh, my! Oh, my!" as they saw them pass by.

Late in the evening, tired and happy and miles from home, they stopped and had supper, sitting on the grass by the roadside.

Toad boasted about all the things he was going to do.

He talked until he was too tired to go on and they all went to bed in their little bunks in the caravan.

Poor Rat was obviously missing the river.

"Shall we run away tomorrow?" whispered Mole.

"No," whispered back Rat. "We'll stick by Toad until this trip is ended. He wouldn't be safe by himself!"

Nor was he safe with Mole and Rat!

Next day, as they were going along the road – Mole leading the horse, and Toad and Rat walking behind the caravan – there was suddenly an imperious "Poop-poop" behind them.

A motor car whizzed by in a cloud of dust and noise. The horse bucked and reared, dragging poor Mole off his feet.

The caravan finished up in the ditch. And Toad finished up sitting in the middle of the road.

It was a long walk for the three animals to the nearest town, where they found somebody to look after the horse and what was left of the caravan.

But Toad wasn't at all upset. He could talk of nothing but that wonderful thing, the motor car, which had caused the accident.

Next evening, when Mole was sitting by the river, fishing, Rat came up. "Heard the news?" he said. "Toad has ordered a large and expensive motor car!"

Chapter 3

THE WILD WOOD

For a long time, Mole had wanted to meet the Badger, but Rat obviously was not keen.

So one day at the beginning of winter, while Rat dozed in front of his fire, Mole set off to explore the Wild Wood, hoping to bump into Mr. Badger.

It was a cold afternoon.

Everything was very still.

It was getting dark.

Then the faces began....

Meanwhile, Rat had been having a lovely warm doze by the fire. When he woke up at last, he called "Moly!" several times.

But there was no answer.

Then he found that Mole's cap was missing from the peg in the hall.

And when he opened the door, he saw Mole's tracks in the mud leading away from the house – straight towards the Wild Wood.

Rat armed himself with a
pair of pistols and a stout
cudgel, and set off bravely
into the Wild Wood.

He searched for over an hour, calling "Moly, Moly,
where are you?"

At last he heard an answering little cry coming from
a hole at the foot of a tree. He looked inside – and
there was Mole.

"Oh Ratty," he cried, "I've been so frightened."

"Now then," said Rat, "we must pull ourselves
together and get going. It would never do to spend the
night here!"

"Dear Ratty," said Mole, "I'm so tired – I must rest
a bit longer."

And Mole snuggled down into the dry leaves and
went to sleep.

Rat now attacked a snow bank beside them. Mole scraped busily too.

Ten minutes hard work and they found a solid little door, painted dark green. Beside it was a brass plate, which read: MR. BADGER.

Mole was chattering away in his excitement, but Rat said, "Get up and hang on to that bell-pull, and ring as hard as you can while I hammer on the door."

Chapter 4

MR. BADGER

At last they heard the sound of slow, shuffling footsteps approaching the door from the inside.

There was a noise of a bolt being shot back, the door opened, and there was Mr. Badger.

"Oh Badger, let us in, please!" cried Rat. "We've lost our way in the snow."

"Come on into the kitchen," said Badger kindly. "There's a fire there and supper."

Badger sat the two of them down by the fireside
and told them to take off their wet coats and boots.

Then he fetched them dressing gowns and slippers
and put some sticking plaster on the cut on Mole's leg.

And, as he started laying the table for a lovely
supper, both Rat and Mole felt they were miles away
from the Wild Wood outside.

After supper they all sat round the fire and talked about Toad's troubles with his new love of driving fast cars – until it was time for bed.

Then Mr. Badger took Rat and Mole up to the spare bedroom in the loft where there were two beds surrounded by all his winter stores.

When they came down to breakfast, very late next morning, Rat and Mole found two young hedgehogs eating porridge out of wooden bowls. They also had been lost in the snow.

And hardly had they all sat down together when there was a clanging of the doorbell, a stamping of feet in the hall, and in rushed Otter.

"They've all been so worried about you on the river bank," he cried.

Soon after breakfast, Mr. Badger sent the two
hedgehogs off home and suggested the others should
stay to lunch.

Mole told him how much he liked living
underground.

"When lunch is over," agreed Mr. Badger, "I'll take
you all round this place of mine."

And, true to his promise, he lit a lantern and
showed Mole all over his house, through narrow
passages, long corridors, vaults and storerooms.

When they got back to the
kitchen again, they found
that Rat was very restless.
"Come on, Mole," he said
anxiously. "We must get off
– we don't want another
night in the Wild Wood."
"It'll be all right,"
said Otter. "I'm coming
with you!"

So they all said goodbye
to Mr. Badger and Otter led
them safely home.

Chapter 5

MR. TOAD

On a bright, sunny morning early in the summer, Mole and Rat had been busy with the boat.

They had been painting and varnishing and mending the paddles; and they were just finishing their breakfast in the parlour when there was a heavy knock on the door.

"Bother!" said Rat, all over egg. "See who it is, Mole, will you?"

It was Mr. Badger.

He strode heavily into the room, looking very, very serious.

"Toad's hour has come," he said solemnly. "This very morning another new and very powerful motor car will arrive at Toad Hall. You two must come with me at once and stop him doing any further harm."

"Right you are!" cried Rat, starting up. "We'll rescue Toad. We'll convert him!"

The three of them set off up the road, and when they reached the carriage drive of Toad Hall, they found a shiny, new, bright red motor car standing in front of the house.

And, just as they arrived, Toad came out dressed in goggles, cap and enormous overcoat.

"Hullo, you fellows," he began cheerfully, "you're just in time to come for a jolly…"

But Rat and Mole grabbed him.

Mr. Badger strode up the steps to the front door. "Take him inside," he said sternly to his companions.

Then he turned to the chauffeur in charge of the new car.

"I'm afraid you won't be wanted today," he said. "Mr. Toad has changed his mind."

And he followed the others inside.

"Now then," said
Mr. Badger to Mole
and Rat.
"Take those silly driving
clothes off him!"

Toad was kicking and struggling, so Rat sat on him
while Mole got the motoring clothes off him bit
by bit.

"You've taken no notice of our warnings," said
Mr. Badger severely. "You're getting us all a bad
name by your furious driving."

"I'll make one more effort to bring you to reason," went on Mr. Badger. "You come with me into the smoking-room."

Three-quarters of an hour later, Mr. Badger reappeared with a limp and tearful Toad.

"He's very sorry and he's going to give up motor cars for ever," announced Mr. Badger.

Mr. Badger asked Toad to repeat in front of his friends what he had just said in the smoking-room.

They all looked at him.

"No!" he said. "I'm not sorry. In fact the first motor car I see, 'poop–poop!' Off I go in it!"

"What," cried Mr. Badger. "You backsliding animal you… Take him upstairs you two, and lock him in his bedroom."

"It's going to be a long business," said Mr. Badger, sighing. "I've never seen Toad so determined."

And true enough, while he was locked in his room, Toad would arrange the bedroom chairs to look like a motor car.

Then he would pretend that he was in the driving seat and drive along – "poop-poop" until he had an accident.

One day, when Mole and Mr. Badger had gone out for a ramble in the woods, Rat went upstairs to see Toad and found him still in bed.

"Ratty," he murmured feebly, "would you go to the village quickly. And fetch a doctor. Even now it may be too late!"

Rat hurried from the room, being very careful, however, to lock the door behind him.

"It's best to be on the safe side," he said to himself.

"I'd better humour him and go," he thought. "If there's nothing really the matter, the doctor will tell him he's an old ass."

So he ran off to the village on his errand of mercy.

Little did he know that Toad had hopped out of bed as soon as he heard the key turn in the lock.

Toad got dressed quickly in his best suit and filled his pockets with money.

Then he took the sheets off his bed. He tied them together and fastened one end to the centre mullion of his window.

He scrambled out of the window, held on to the sheets very tightly, and slid gently to the ground below.

Taking the opposite direction
to Rat, Toad scampered off
happily, whistling a merry tune.

Poor Rat felt a terrible fool when Mr. Badger and
Mole came back and he had to tell them that Toad
had escaped.

"You've been a bit of a duffer this time, Ratty," said
Mole. "Toad, too, of all animals!"

"He did it awfully well," said Rat.

Meanwhile, Toad, gay and irresponsible, walked briskly along.

"Smart piece of work that," he said to himself, chuckling.

And when he reached a little town, he went into the hotel and ordered a slap-up lunch for himself to celebrate his escape.

He was half-way through his meal when he heard a "poop-poop" and a motor car stopping outside.

The occupants came inside, and Toad could contain himself no longer. Out into the yard he went to have a look.

"I wonder if this sort of car *starts* easily," he murmured.

Of course, Toad just could not resist the temptation.

He got in, started the engine and drove out of the yard.

He drove out of the town and sped through the open country beyond.

He felt that he was Toad once more, Toad at his best, Toad the terror, the traffic-queller.

The miles were eaten up under him as he went. He knew not whither, living his hour, reckless of what might come to him…

"Let me see," said the Magistrate. "He is guilty of stealing a motor car, of driving dangerously and of cheeking the police. What's the stiffest penalty we can give him?"

"Twenty years," said the Clerk.
"Excellent!" said the Magistrate.

52

So poor Toad was taken off to prison, loaded with chains.

They had to drag him from the courthouse, shrieking and protesting; past the crowds in the market-place and across the drawbridge of the grim old castle.

They took the unhappy Toad past sentries and guardrooms full of grinning soldiers. They led him right to the door of the grimmest dungeon that lay in the heart of the innermost keep in the castle.

The rusty key creaked in the lock, the great door clanged behind him, and Toad was a helpless prisoner.

Chapter 6

TOAD'S ADVENTURES

Chained up in his dungeon, all alone, Toad shed bitter tears and abandoned himself to despair.

"This is the end of everything," he wept. "How can I ever hope to be free again?"

And for several weeks he refused all the food brought to him by the grim and ancient gaoler.

But the gaoler had a daughter, a good-hearted girl who helped her father sometimes in the prison.

She was very fond of animals and she said to her father one day: "I can't bear to see poor Toad so unhappy and getting so thin."

"Let me look after him," she pleaded.

"Do what you like," said the gaoler.

So that very day, the gaoler's daughter went to see Toad, to talk to him and to tempt him with food.

At first he would not be comforted, but when she brought him tea and very thick hot buttered toast he started eating again.

And they had many interesting talks together.

She told him that she had an elderly aunt who was the washerwoman at the prison.

She suggested that, if Toad gave this lady a little money, she might be willing to let him have one of her dresses and an old bonnet so that he could escape from the castle.

And so, next morning, the girl brought her aunt to Toad's cell.

Shaking with laughter, the gaoler's daughter helped Toad to dress up in the cotton print gown, arranged the shawl and tied on the washerwoman's bonnet; all of which her aunt had brought in her bundle of washing.

Then the pair of them tied the old lady up to make it look as though the daring Toad had overpowered her to steal the clothes.

With quaking heart but firm footstep, Toad made his way through the castle.

The warders and the soldiers joked as they saw the stout little figure in familiar clothes go walking by.

Every door and every gate was opened for him.

Even so, it seemed hours before he crossed the last courtyard – and then he was walking across the drawbridge.

Free!

Dizzy with the success of his daring exploit, Toad made his way to the railway station.

He went to the booking office to buy a ticket – and found to his horror that he had left all his money and belongings behind in the prison.

He pleaded with the booking-clerk, but he was pushed out of the way.

In despair again, he wandered down the platform to where the train was waiting. He told the engine driver all his troubles.

Luckily, the engine driver was a very kind man. He told the poor washerwoman that if she washed a few shirts for him she could have a lift in his cab.

Toad was very thrilled as the train sped along.

But after a while, the engine driver said they were being followed by another engine.

"And it's crowded with warders and policemen," he exclaimed.

So he slowed down enough for Toad to jump off as they passed through a thick wood.

He rolled down an embankment and scrambled into the wood. He watched his train get up speed again and disappear.

Then the pursuing engine roared past, everybody shouting, "Stop! Stop!"

Toad had a hearty laugh for the first time since he was thrown into prison.

Chapter 7

THE FURTHER ADVENTURES OF TOAD

Toad slept that night in the hollow of a tree. He woke up next morning because his toes were cold.

But he soon forgot about that when he remembered that he was free!

He had all the world to himself that early summer morning and he strolled along the lanes until he came to a canal.

Round a bend in the canal came plodding a large horse, towing a barge. Steering the barge was a large, stout woman.

"A nice morning, Ma'am," she called to Toad as the barge drew level with him.

Toad replied politely and said that he was a poor washerwoman trying to get back to her home near Toad Hall.

"Toad Hall?" answered the barge-woman. "Why,
I'm going that way."

"Toad's luck again!" thought Toad as he stepped
lightly on board the barge. "I always come out
on top."

But there was a surprise in store for Toad
this time!

"You can get on with my washing
for me," said the barge-woman.

He had travelled a long way when he came to a gipsy caravan where a man was sitting by a fire of sticks.

From the pot which was hanging over the fire came the most delicious smells.

Toad just sat there and sniffed hungrily.

"Want to sell that horse of yours?" asked the gipsy.

"Sell this beautiful horse?" exclaimed Toad. "Oh, no – it's out of the question."

But the gipsy continued to bargain with him and offered fifty pence.

Toad thought very carefully. He *was* very hungry and he had no money.

"Look here, gipsy," he said. "If you give me seventy-five pence, plus as much as I can possibly eat out of that pot, you shall have my horse."

So it was arranged and Toad stuffed and stuffed and kept asking for more.

After he had finished eating, Toad set off for the road once more, very pleased with himself.

He saw a car approaching and stood in the middle of the road to stop it.

But, oh dear! as it slowed down he recognised it as the car he had stolen.

Poor Toad collapsed in despair in the road.

Toad thought that the people in the car would send for the police.

But, no. All they saw was a poor old washerwoman lying in the road, and they decided to take her to the nearest village.

So they lifted Toad into the car and as they moved off his courage began to revive.

And when they had gone a little way, he asked if he could drive the car!

How they laughed! "Let the old lady try!"

Toad eagerly took the wheel and drove off, very slowly at first, then faster and faster.

And when he started boasting what a clever Toad he was, they realised their mistake and tried to grab him.

The car went through a hedge and they all landed in a muddy pool.

Chapter 8

'LIKE SUMMER TEMPEST

CAME HIS TEARS'

Toad ran off as fast as he could go, chased by the men from the car.

He was looking back over his shoulder when – SPLASH – he ran straight into the river!

Breathless and spluttering, he floated along a little way with the stream and presently he saw a big dark hole in the river bank.

It was Rat's house – and Rat was there to rescue him.

As soon as Toad was indoors, he started boasting to Rat about his adventures.

"Toad," said Rat gravely, "You go upstairs and take off that old cotton rag and put on some of my clothes.

Now stop swaggering and arguing! I'll have something to say to you later."

Toad washed and changed his clothes and stood looking at himself in the mirror with pride and pleasure.

Feeling much better, he went downstairs and ate a large lunch prepared by Rat. When they had both finished eating, Rat told him how the Stoats and the Weasels had taken over Toad Hall.

"I'll jolly well soon see about that!" said Toad, grabbing a stick and marching rapidly down the road to Toad Hall.

But when he got to the front gate, a yellow ferret with a gun suddenly popped out and fired at Toad.

BANG! And a bullet whistled over his head.

But Toad was not going to give in.

He went back to Rat's house.

He got out the boat.

And he rowed up the river towards Toad Hall. All seemed peaceful and quiet until – CRASH! – a great stone, thrown from the bridge, smashed through the bottom of the boat and it sank!

Toad struggled back to tell Rat all about it. And Rat prepared a big supper for him.

Just as they finished, there was a knock at the door – and there was Mr. Badger.

He solemnly shook Toad by the paw.

"This is a poor homecoming," he said. "Unhappy Toad."

A little while later, Mole arrived too and they talked about the situation.

Badger said, "The stoats are on guard at every point. It's quite useless to think of attacking the place. They're too strong for us."

"Then it's all over," sobbed Toad. "I shall never see my dear Toad Hall any more…"

"Cheer up, Toady," cried Badger encouragingly. "I'm going to tell you a secret. There is an underground passage from the river bank that leads right into the middle of Toad Hall – and there's a banquet there tomorrow night."

"We shall creep out quietly…" cried Mole.

"With pistols and swords…" shouted Rat.

"And whack 'em and whack 'em," cried Toad in ecstasy.

Next morning, Toad slept till late. When he did
come down to breakfast, he found that Rat was
collecting swords and pistols.

The Badger said that all they would need was sticks,
once they got into Toad Hall.

"It's as well to be on the safe side," said Rat.

Then Mole came in.

He told them that he had been up to Toad Hall dressed in the old washer-woman's dress. He had spoken to the guards and told them that all the animals were going to attack Toad Hall from the *outside*.

"Oh, you silly ass, Mole!" cried Toad. "You've been and spoilt everything!"

But Badger could see the sense in what Mole had done. "Good Mole!" he said approvingly.

This made Toad a bit jealous, especially because he could not make out what it was that Mole had done that was so clever.

So Mole took him outside, and made Toad tell him about all his adventures from beginning to end.

Chapter 9

THE RETURN OF ULYSSES

hen it began to grow dark, they all assembled in Rat's parlour, and Rat gave each one his sword and pistols.

But Badger just laughed good-humouredly.

"I'm going to do all I've got to do with this here stick," he said.

When they were ready, Badger took a lantern and led them along by the river and then into a hole in the river bank.

Mole and Rat followed silently, but when it came to Toad's turn, of course he managed to slip and fell into the water.

He was hauled out by his friends, but Badger was very cross.

A little while later, they were creeping along the secret passage, which was dark and cold and damp.

Toad was hurrying to keep up with the others when he bumped into Rat, who bumped into Mole, who fell over.

Badger thought they were being attacked from behind and he very nearly shot Toad with his pistol.

After that, Rat kept a firm grip on Toad's shoulder to keep him out of trouble. And so they groped and shuffled along the secret passage until they came to a trap door.

Badger said, "Now, boys, all together!"

They found themselves in the pantry with only a door between them and the banqueting hall.

They could hear the Weasels cheering and singing.

Badger cried, "Follow me!" and he flung the door open wide.

My!

What a squealing and a squeaking and a screeching filled the air!

Mole had gone outside to deal with the sentries.

"It's all over," he reported back. "They had been expecting an attack from outside, but as soon as they heard the shrieks and yells inside the hall, they threw down their rifles and fled."

"They've all disappeared by now, and I've got their rifles."

And so the four friends sat down to a great supper of chicken and jelly and trifle.

After all this excitement, the four animals continued to be friends. They would often take a stroll together in the Wild Wood and it was pleasing to see how the mother weasels would bring out their young ones and point them out.

"There goes the great Mr. Toad,
and the gallant Water Rat, and the
famous Mr. Mole," they would say.

And, when their children were
naughty, they would tell them that
the terrible grey Badger would
come and get them if they didn't
behave themselves. Which was a
little unfair on Badger because he
was rather fond of children.

But it never failed!